Fancy NANCY

Sand Castles and Sand Palaces

Based on *Fancy Nancy* written by Jane O'Connor

Cover illustration by Robin Preiss Glasser

Interior illustrations by Carolyn Bracken

HARPER FESTIVAL

An Imprint of HarperCollins*Publishers*

HarperFestival is an imprint of HarperCollins Publishers.

Fancy Nancy: Sand Castles and Sand Palaces
For information address HarperCollins Children's Books, a division of HarperCollins Publishers, 10 East 53rd Street, New York, NY 10022.
www.harpercollinschildrens.com
Library of Congress catalog card number: 2013950290
ISBN 978-0-06-226954-6
Book design by Sean Boggs
14 15 16 17 18 CWM 10 9 8 7 6 5 4 3 2 1
❖
First Edition

Ooh la la! We are going on an outing—that's fancy for a short trip.

Can you guess where we are headed? If you think it's the beach, you are one hundred percent correct!

The car ride takes forever. The traffic is terrible, awful, and horrendous!

Now we have to stop at a gas station because JoJo needs to use the lavatory. (That's fancy for bathroom.)

Right away we run down to the ocean and frolic in the waves.
Frolic is fancy for jumping around and having fun.

Then it's time for refreshments. Why does everything taste better at the beach? Maybe it's because of the salty air.

Now we get down to serious business— building the fanciest sand castle ever.

My mom shows us how to decorate the towers. You hold wet sand in your fist and let it dribble out from the bottom.

Voilà! Doesn't it look gorgeous?

We decorate the walls with shells.

"Check it out!" Bree says, and giggles. "My shell is crawling away."

We dig a moat all the way around the castle.

"This isn't a sand castle," I say. "It's a sand palace."

After so much hard work, we all agree that more frolicking in the waves is what we need.

But soon my mom says that the waves are getting too big.
We have to come out.

Oh, no! Look what one of the waves did. Our sand palace is in ruins!

JoJo starts crying, but I am more mature. That's because I have been to the beach many times before. "The beach never runs out of sand or shells," I tell my sister. "We can build an even bigger and better sand palace."

So that is exactly what we do.